To my resilient daughter who never wavered
even when Mommy had no hair, to my amazing
caretakers, and to all of the other mommies
whose strength will define them, not their hair!

www.mascotbooks.com

Still My Mommy

©2016 Megan Pomputius. All Rights Reserved. No part of this publication
may be reproduced, stored in a retrieval system or transmitted in any
form by any means electronic, mechanical, or photocopying, recording or
otherwise without the permission of the author.

For more information, please contact:
Mascot Books
560 Herndon Parkway #120
Herndon, VA 20170
info@mascotbooks.com

Library of Congress Control Number: 2016900207

CPSIA Code: PRT0216A
ISBN: 978-1-63177-518-5

Printed in the United States

Still My Mommy

by Megan Pomputius
art by Andrea Alemanno

My mommy likes to put me on her feet and fly me high up in the sky like Supergirl. She says, "You're strong like a mountain, you're fierce like a tiger, and you can take on the world!"

We read our favorite books together and she teaches me how to write my letters. She lets me paint pretty pictures and sometimes we even get to paint with our fingers!

We turn on the sprinkler in the back yard and she holds my hand tight as we run as fast as we can through the water spraying all around.

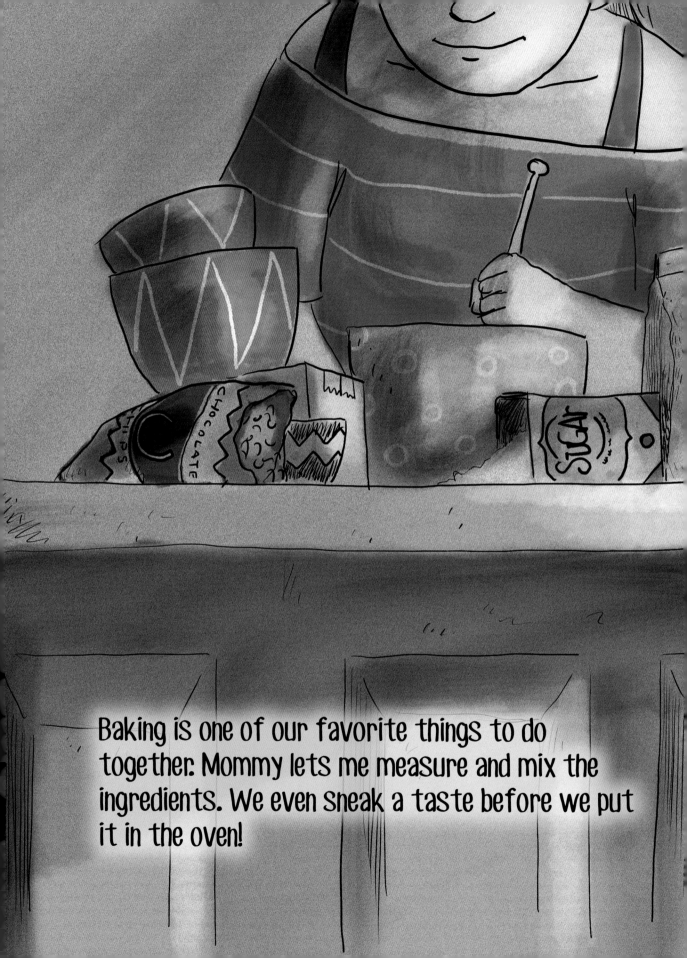

Baking is one of our favorite things to do together. Mommy lets me measure and mix the ingredients. We even sneak a taste before we put it in the oven!

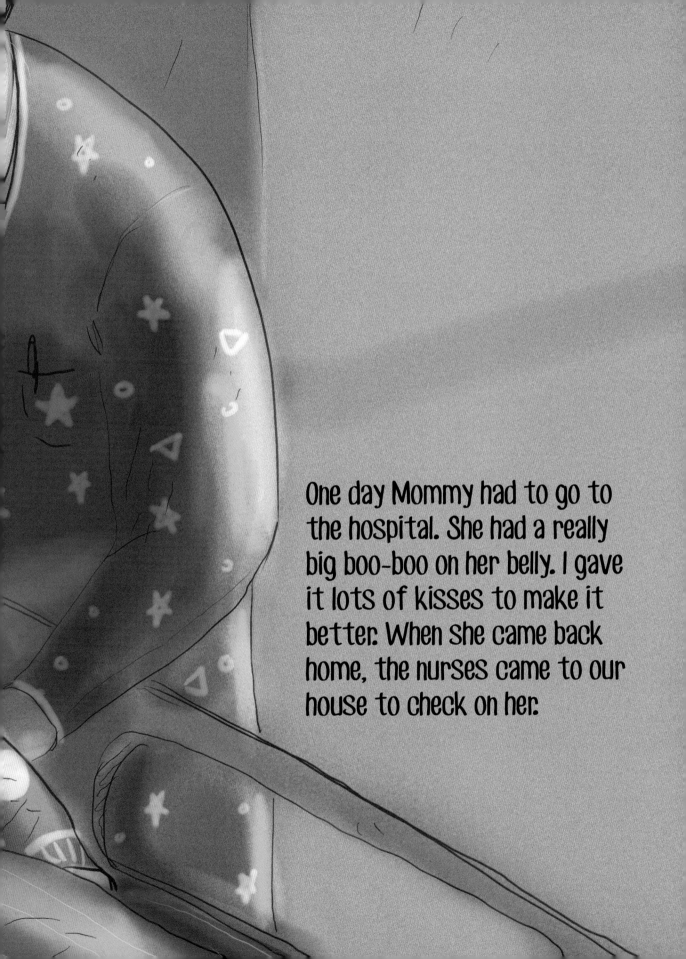

One day Mommy had to go to the hospital. She had a really big boo-boo on her belly. I gave it lots of kisses to make it better. When she came back home, the nurses came to our house to check on her.

They checked her heartbeat and made her breathe in and out, in and out. I practiced on my dolls too, just in case Mommy needed my help. I told them, "In and out, baby. Breathe in and out."

"Mommy is sick," Daddy told me. "She has to take medicine for a long time. It will make her very tired and make her lose all of her hair, too."

"I already know how to take care of her," I told Daddy. "I'll bring her blankets, wrap her nice and tight, and kiss her boo-boo to make her feel better."

Soon Mommy's hair started falling out. It looked really funny, so I watched as Daddy cut all of Mommy's hair off with the clippers. She looked different but I knew she was still my mommy.

We visited a fancy salon where Mommy got to try on all different hairstyles.

Brown ones, blonde ones, curly ones, and even a blue one! She let me try them on, too!

Some days, Mommy is really tired
and just lies on the couch.

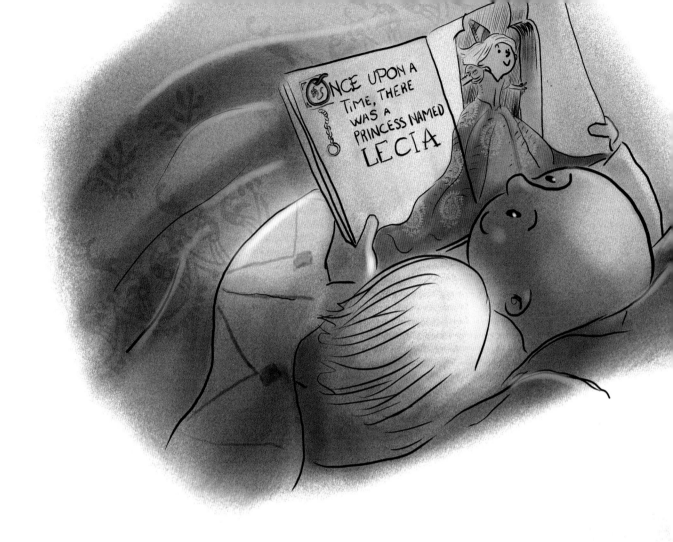

I cuddle up next to her and she says it helps her feel better. She still reads me my favorite bedtime stories, and even makes one up where I'm the princess of the castle!

Even though Mommy looks different without her hair, she is still my mommy. She is strong, she is fierce, and she can take on the world!

About the Author

Megan is the wife of Dustin, mommy of Lecia and Titan the pit bull. She lives in Pennsylvania with her family and teaches fourth grade at St. Bernard School. She is an ovarian cancer survivor and hopes that this story will bring hope and comfort to others facing cancer in their lives.

Have a book idea?

Contact us at:

**Mascot Books
560 Herndon Parkway
Suite 120
Herndon, VA 20170**

info@mascotbooks.com | www.mascotbooks.com